Best wishes

Nicholas Allan

Nicholas Allan

HUTCHINSON
London Sydney Auckland Johannesburg

To Bill Hamilton

First published in 1998

1 3 5 7 9 10 8 6 4 2

© Nicholas Allan 1998

Nicholas Allan has asserted his right under
the Copyright, Designs and Patents Act, 1988,
to be identified as the author and illustrator of this work

First published in the United Kingdom in 1998
Hutchinson Children's Books
Random House UK Limited
20 Vauxhall Bridge Road, London SW1V 2SA

Random House Australia (Pty) Limited
20 Alfred Street, Milsons Point, Sydney
New South Wales 2061, Australia

Random House New Zealand Limited
18 Poland Road, Glenfield
Auckland 10, New Zealand

Random House South Africa (Pty) Limited
Endulini, 5A Jubilee Road, Parktown 2193, South Africa

Random House UK Limited Reg. No. 954009

A CIP catalogue record for this book is available from the British Library

ISBN: 0 09 176749 0

Printed in Singapore

This is Jesus.

Bartholomew Andrew Philip Simon Judas Matth

These are his friends.

eter Thomas Judas John James James
Iscariot

He had twelve of them.

Jesus could do amazing miracles,
and no one could work out
how they were done.

Each day he worked hard to make

everything around him beautiful . . .

. . . until one day he woke up exhausted from saving the world.

That day
the miracles
didn't go quite
so well . . .

. . . nor
did the stories.

The next morning Jesus went to the doctor.
After examining him the doctor advised,
'Take the day off, Jesus. Relax. Enjoy yourself.
Sit in the sun.'

So Jesus told his friends what the doctor
had ordered, and then went out for a walk.
It was a lovely cloudless day.

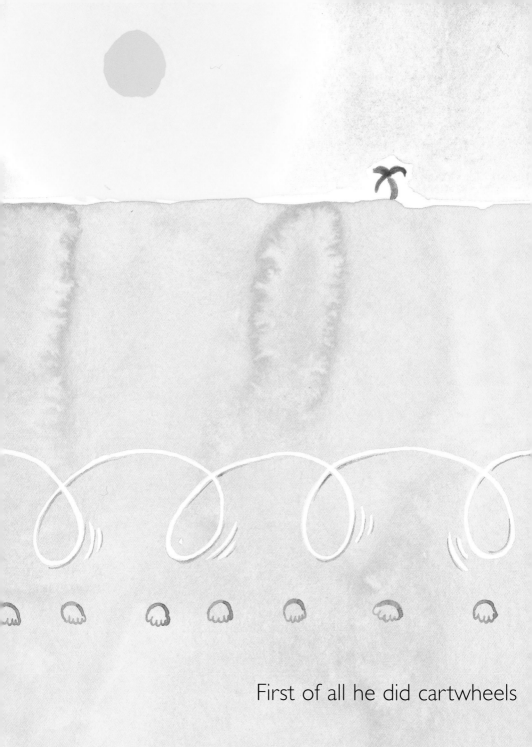

First of all he did cartwheels

right across the desert.

Then he played catch with his halo.

Then he had a picnic.

After that he had a refreshing swim.

And finally he went on a long donkey ride —
something he always enjoyed.

Jesus loved his dad
very much. Dad knew
everything, and always
had the right thing
to say.

When Jesus told him about his day off,
his dad said, 'Look down there a minute, son.'
So Jesus looked down.

'Where you did your cartwheels, fountains of water appeared in the desert...

...where you threw your halo and ate your picnic, the trees bloomed with fruit...

...when you went swimming, the fishermen had lots of luck...

...and whoever you passed on your donkey, felt instantly happy.'

'So you see, when you're feeling better yourself, you can only make others feel better too.'

Jesus knew that, as usual, his father was right.

'Thanks, dad,' he said.

When Jesus got home his friends were
so happy to see him looking so well, they
cooked him a delicious supper.

The end